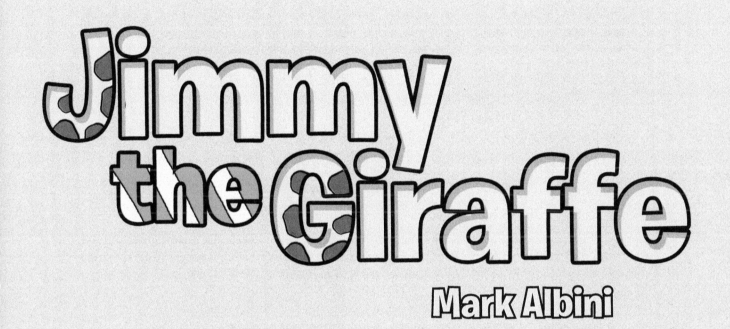

Jimmy the Giraffe

Mark Albini

Archway Publishing books may be ordered through booksellers or by contacting:

Archway Publishing
1663 Liberty Drive
Bloomington, IN 47403
www.archwaypublishing.com
1 (888) 242-5904

Because of the dynamic nature of the Internet, any web addresses or links contained in this book may have changed since publication and may no longer be valid. The views expressed in this work are solely those of the author and do not necessarily reflect the views of the publisher, and the publisher hereby disclaims any responsibility for them.

Any people depicted in stock imagery provided by Thinkstock are models, and such images are being used for illustrative purposes only.
Certain stock imagery © Thinkstock.

ISBN: 978-1-4808-3098-1 (sc)
ISBN: 978-1-4808-3099-8 (hc)
ISBN: 978-1-4808-3100-1 (e)

Print information available on the last page.

Archway Publishing rev. date: 6/27/2016

INTRODUCTION

The Rescue Ranch is a peaceful place
where animals live in wide open space.
They're fed everyday and have plenty to eat.
Life on this farm is really quite sweet.
It's a place for animals to come and stay
and meet new friends and have fun each day.
The animals are friendly and very sincere
and most have retired from a long career.
Except for those who were born on the farm
and a few in the woods that have caused alarm
If they live in the woods or somewhere on the farm
they all contribute to its countryside charm.
So welcome to the Rescue Ranch
where animals receive an olive branch.

Jimmy the Giraffe woke up a little late.

He got ready for school and rushed out the gate.

He walked by a shed as he did everyday

and joined Howie the Horse for a quick bale of hay.
It wasn't much of a meal, just a mouthful of hay.
But to Jimmy and Howie it was like a buffet.

They ate the whole bale and they ate it so quick that Jimmy the Giraffe began to feel sick.

Then Howie saw something on Jimmy's neck
and Howie told Jimmy he'd better go check.

So Jimmy ran off to look in the mirror and found he had dirt up his neck to his ear.

So Jimmy asked Howie to go get a pail to
clean Jimmy up from his head to his tail.
But Howie said "No, I'm going to be late. Schools
over at three and you'll just have to wait".

Jimmy wanted to leave and join Howie at school
but his neck was so dirty that he'd look like a fool.

So Jimmy was thinking as he walked on the range,
I don't like my long neck and I wish I could change.

It's so hard to get clean when I can't reach my head.
Why I think I would rather be a horse instead.

He walked back in the barn and lay down to sleep
and took a short nap and heard not a peep.

When out of his dream came a voice in the night.
Twas a grey little mouse who was holding a light.

What is your name and why are you here?
This barn's been my home for more than a year.

My name is Jimmy and I'm a giraffe.
I've been waiting for Howie to help with my bath.
I don't like to get wet and I don't want you to laugh
but I'd rather be a horse than I would a giraffe.

Then Bobo asked Jimmy why he was so sure. You may change your mind once you grow and mature. Life's tough on the farm when you work all the day and when it is over they pay you in hay.

You'll pull a steel plow and you'll sweat in the sun.
That's why work on the farm's not a whole lot of fun.

I thought life on the farm would be kind of nice.
But Bobo the Mouse sure made me think twice.
I continued to dream as I lay on the floor and
waited for Howie to come through the door.

Then all of the sudden I heard my good pal.
It was Howie the Horse standing by the corral.

A pail with a brush he held tight in his teeth and Bobo the Mouse held a hose from beneath.

Jimmy was happy to have a clean neck and it gave him some time to think and reflect.

Becoming a horse or pretending to be
led Jimmy to think "I'd just rather be me".
Soon Jimmy grew tired of being a horse.
A happy giraffe would be better of course.

CPSIA information can be obtained
at www.ICGtesting.com
Printed in the USA
LVOW06s2042210716
497299LV00004B/5/P